Dragon

Happy Valentine's Day!

Adapted by Gabrielle Reyes
Based on an original TV episode
written by Greg Dummett & Aline Gilmore

SCHOLASTIC INC.
New York Toronto London Auckland
Sydney Mexico City New Delhi Hong Kong

ISBN 978-0-545-20055-4

Published by Scholastic Inc. SCHOLASTIC and associated logos are trademarks and/or registered trademarks of Scholastic Inc. Lexile is a registered trademark of MetaMetrics, Inc.

12 11 10 9 8 7 6 5 4 3 2 1 10 11 12 13 14/0

Printed in the U.S.A. 40
First printing, December 2010

“Today is Valentine’s Day!” said Dragon.
“I hope I get some valentines
from my friends.”

"Hello, Dragon!" said Mailmouse.
"I have lots of mail for you."

Dragon's friends had sent him cards for Valentine's Day.

Now Dragon wanted to show his friends how much he loved them.

“I have an idea!” said Dragon.
“I will bake cookies for them.”

The baking cookies smelled yummy!
Dragon was getting hungry.

“But the cookies are for my friends!”
said Dragon.
“I cannot eat them.”

He tried to stop smelling
the yummy smell.

At last the cookies were done!

Dragon put the cookies on a plate to cool.

Then he spotted a crumb on the table.
“I can eat one tiny crumb,” said Dragon.

It tasted so good.
Dragon shook the plate until
another crumb fell.
And he ate that one too.
Soon there were no crumbs left!

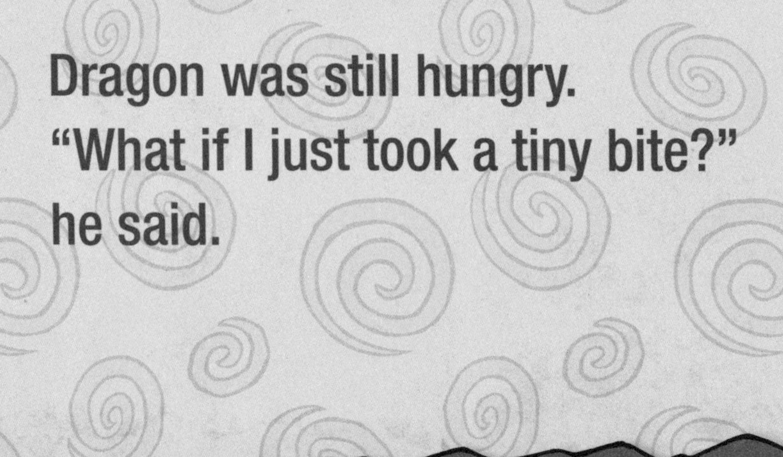

Dragon was still hungry.
"What if I just took a tiny bite?"
he said.

So he took one tiny bite.

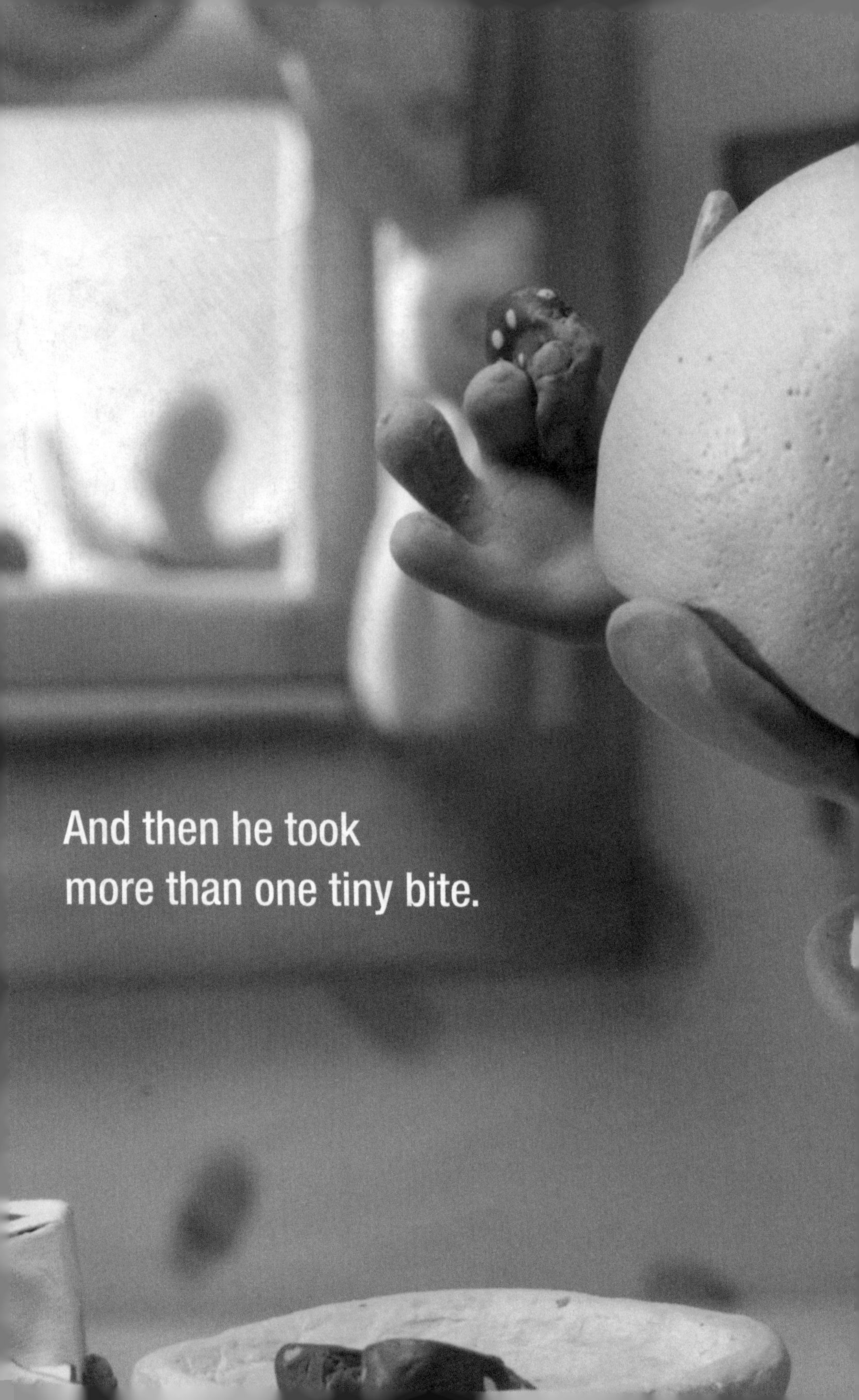

And then he took
more than one tiny bite.

Soon there were no cookies left!

“Oh no,” said Dragon.
“Now what will I do for my friends?”

Dragon had a new idea.

First he took some rocks.
Then he picked some red flowers.

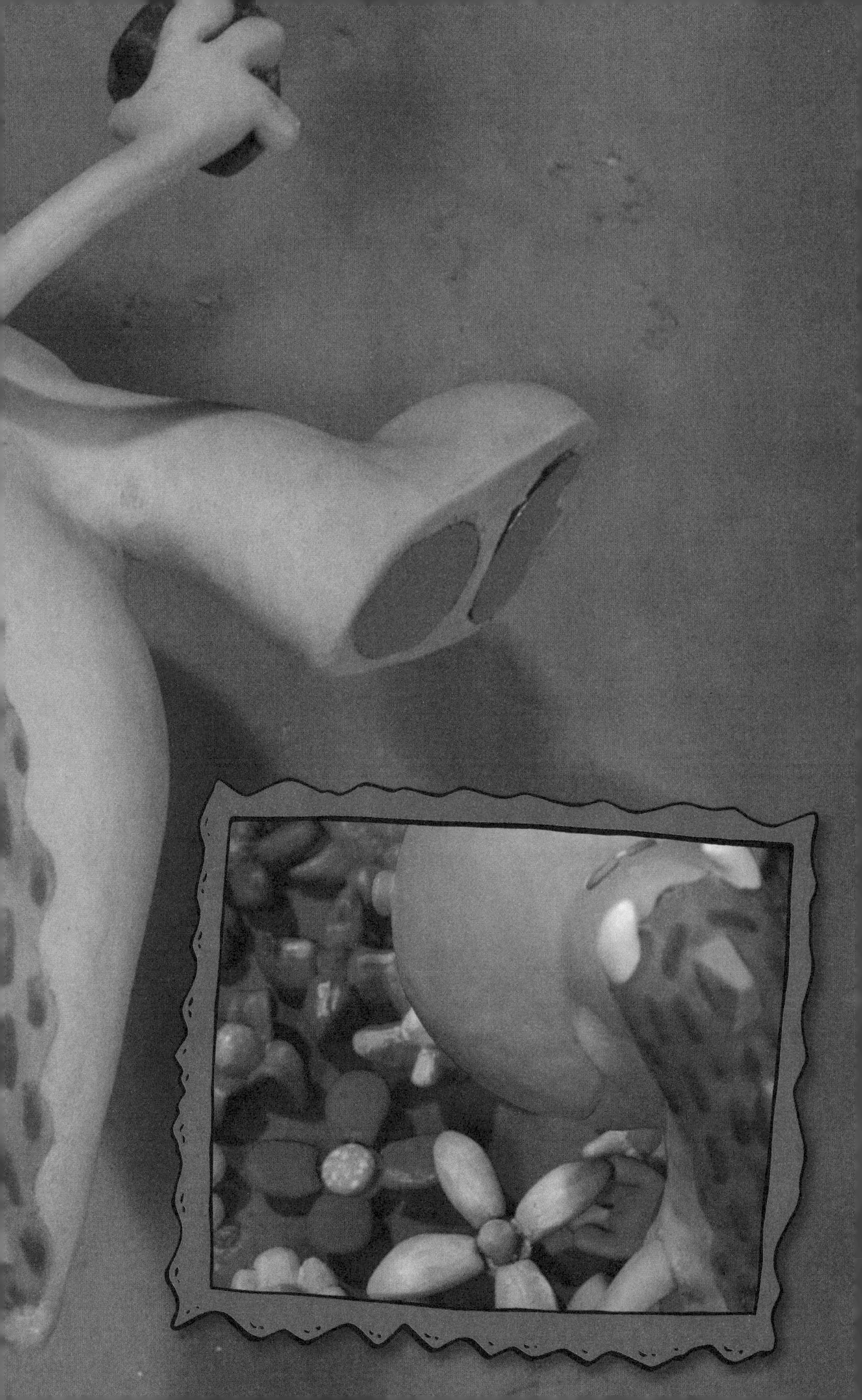

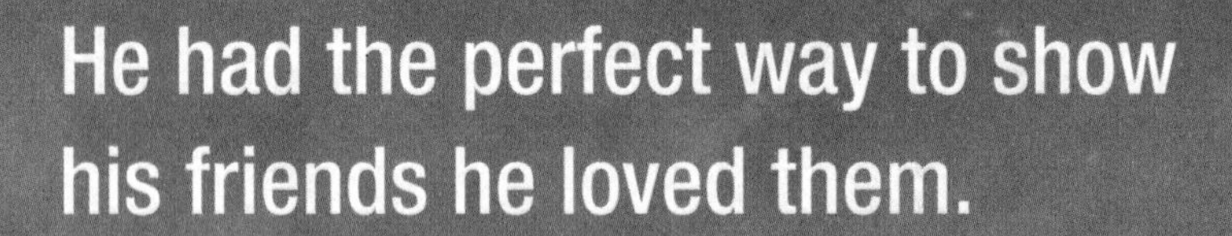

He had the perfect way to show
his friends he loved them.

Happy Valentine's Day!